T3-ADB-794

How Rabbit
Lost His Tail

How Rabbit
Lost His Tail

A Traditional Cherokee Legend

A Grandmother Story

Drawings by
Murv Jacob

Story by
Deborah L. Duvall

University of New Mexico Press
Albuquerque

T 104532

This book is dedicated to two of our favorite friends,

John D. Loudermilk and Rita Coolidge, the storyteller and the singer.

© 2003 University of New Mexico Press

First edition

All rights reserved.

Library of Congress Cataloging-in-Publication

Duvall, Deborah L., 1952–

How rabbit lost his tail : a traditional Cherokee legend / drawings by Murv Jacob ; story by Deborah L. Duvall.— 1st ed.

p.   cm.   — (The grandmother stories ; v. 3)

Summary: When Rabbit becomes jealous of Otter's beautiful coat, which causes his own

beautiful tail to be ignored, he plots to steal the coat and become popular again.

ISBN 0-8263-3010-X (cloth : alk. paper)

1. Rabbit (Legendary character)   2. Cherokee Indians—Folklore.   3. Tales—Southern States.

[1. Rabbit (Legendary character)   2. Cherokee Indians—Folklore.   3. Indians of North America—Folklore.]

I. Jacob, Murv, ill.   II. Title.   III. Series.

E99.C5 D89 2003

398.24'52939'0899755—dc21

2003006024

Design by Melissa Tandysh

Printed in Japan

Rabbit, whose name is Ji-Stu,
    was in a big hurry.

He walked down the path into the forest as fast as he could go. That night all the animals would meet at the dance grounds and he could not be late.

The path to the dance grounds followed the river that ran through the Cherokee lands. In some places where the river curved, the water formed deep pools that reflected the river bank above. Each time he passed such a pool, Ji-Stu stopped just long enough to look at his reflection, for he was very proud. He was proud of his shiny eyes and his long floppy ears. But mostly he was proud of his tail.

Ji-Stu's tail was long and beautiful and covered with plenty of thick silky fur that gleamed even in the moonlight. It gleamed in the reflecting pool as he gazed down at it. Ji-Stu took a moment to comb his magnificent tail before rushing on down the path to the dance.

"Si-yo, Yona, hello," Ji-Stu greeted the great Bear who tended the fire. "Have you noticed how beautiful my tail looks this evening?"

"Hah!" Yona laughed in reply. "Everyone has seen your tail and heard you brag about it too many times. But no one will notice you tonight! Look over there."

Ji-Stu turned his eyes to the crowd of animals that had gathered near the pathway. He hurried over to see what they could be looking at. The others never noticed him or his beautiful tail as he scrambled between them for a better view.

Down the forest path walked an unusual creature with a happy smiling face. The girl animals giggled and blushed as the latest arrival made his way to the dance grounds. To Ji-Stu's dismay, he realized that it was Otter, who was famous far and wide for his exquisite shiny coat.

For hours Otter danced in turn with all the girls around the fire. Ji-Stu sat on a stump and watched. Once in a while the girls would dance with him, but their eyes would follow the splendid coat of Otter as he whirled and turned in the firelight. Ji-Stu had never taken such a blow and his pride was hurting.

His old friend Possum noticed poor Ji-Stu's suffering and said, "Don't worry, Ji-Stu. Otter may have a pretty coat, but you still have the most beautiful tail in the forest. What I would give to have a tail such as yours!"

But nothing could console Ji-Stu. He had always been the most popular of all the dancers. Never had he been outdone by any other creature. Now he looked down at his tail and it did not seem so beautiful. Nothing seemed beautiful in all the world except Otter's sleek and shiny coat.

Otter lived so far up the river that he was seldom seen in the forest. His appearance at the dance caused the other animals to argue about who among them had the most beautiful coat. The animals agreed to hold a special council and decide this once and for all.

They set the date for three nights later. This would give Otter time to make the journey and appear at the council. The animals planned to save a special seat just for him so that all could see his shiny coat.

Ji-Stu the Rabbit is one of the quickest of all the forest creatures. He is known as "the Messenger," and he was chosen by the animals to carry the news of the council to Otter.

"It is I who should be honored for my beautiful tail," he thought to himself as he bounded toward his home in the broom grass meadow.

Ji-Stu built a fire outside his house that night and cooked up his supper and a pot of tea. He sat for a long time looking at the fire and thinking hard. How could he be chosen by the animal council as the one with the most beautiful coat?

He thought until the moon and stars were bright in the sky, but still no answer came. Hot red coals were all that remained of his cooking fire. Ji-Stu took a stick and poked at the embers. Just then a huge shooting star went streaking across the night sky.

Ji-Stu looked from the glowing trail in the sky to the glowing coals of the fire and an idea began to form in his mind. He knew now what he would do. Tired and sleepy, he closed the door to his little house and jumped into bed. Ji-Stu dreamed all night of falling stars and Otter's coat.

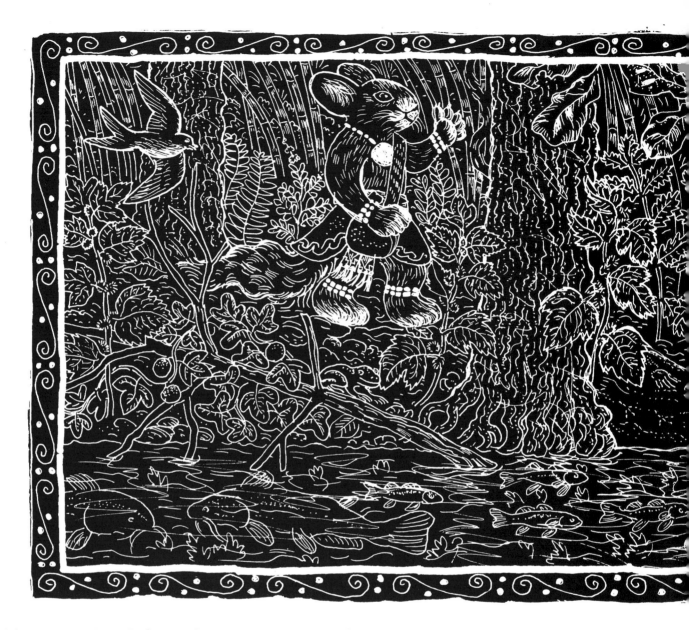

The next day, Ji-Stu left his house just after lunch and headed up the river to Otter's home. Along the way, he swished his fluffy tail and sang happy songs to himself. Soon he came upon Otter, who was fishing on the river bank.

"Si-yo, Otter," Ji-Stu called. "How are you doing today? There is a special animal council in the forest three nights from now. Come to my house tomorrow and walk there with me."

Ji-Stu did not mention the reason for the council or that Otter would sit as an honored guest. But Otter agreed to meet Ji-Stu. He looked forward to another trip into the forest.

"Oh, yes," Ji-Stu said on his way down the path. "We will camp out by the river tomorrow night at a special place I know."

Otter showed up early the next morning and found Ji-Stu pacing around in his house. Ji-Stu could hardly wait to leave and he greeted Otter happily. Together they set off down the path by the river.

Along the way, Ji-Stu gathered sticks and wood and carried them in a pack on his back. Otter wondered why he worked so hard.

"These will warm us in our camp tonight," Ji-Stu explained. "We must build a fire that will last until morning."

Then Ji-Stu found a short pole and shaved it down into the shape of a paddle. Otter wondered about this, too.

"Sleeping with a paddle under my head brings me good luck," Ji-Stu told him as they walked on in the fading light. "I do it all the time."

"Here we are," Ji-Stu said just as darkness fell. "This is that special place I told you about. We will camp here tonight."

They took Ji-Stu's pack of wood and built a big campfire on the river bank. Ji-Stu cooked a tasty supper and boiled some roots for hot tea. It was about time to put his plan to work.

"This is the place where fire falls from the sky," he said at last to Otter, who gazed warily up through the treetops.

"You never know when it might happen," said Ji-Stu. "I just wanted to warn you in case it should happen tonight. If you see fire falling, you must dive in the river and swim far away!"

"Oh, here. Give me your coat," Ji-Stu continued. "I'll hang it on this branch where it will be safe, just in case."

Even though Otter was afraid, he was too tired to stay awake and watch the sky. He handed his coat to Ji-Stu and lay down to rest. Soon he was fast asleep on the river bank, curled up close to the campfire.

While Otter lay dreaming, Ji-Stu stayed awake. He waited until the fire burned down to glowing coals. Taking the paddle he had carved that afternoon, he scooped it full of the red hot coals. Then with a mighty heave he pitched them high into the air.

"Fire is falling from the sky!" He screamed as the coals rained down. "Otter! Swim as fast as you can!"

Otter jumped up and yelled. Through the blaze of red hailstones he ran and dived into the river. Otter swam away, as fast as he could go.

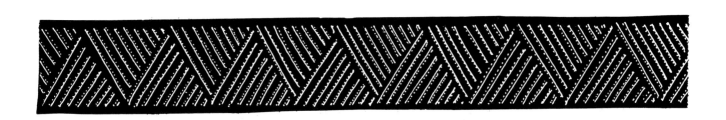

Ji-Stu jumped up and down, laughing with glee, as he thought how Otter looked, swimming like a sleek fish toward his home upstream. He would not return any time soon. On the tree branch hung Otter's gleaming coat. Ji-Stu grabbed it, wrapping it around himself, and the coat kept him warm and snug until morning.

"How wonderful my new coat looks, so shiny and dark, against my fluffy tail," Ji-Stu bragged, looking into the river at his reflection. "Surely the council of animals will choose me tonight."

Ji-Stu took a piece of rawhide and tied his long ears down under his chin. Except for his tail, he did not look at all like his old self. But what could he do about his little split nose? He thought for a while.

"I'll just keep my nose covered with my paw," he decided. "Now I had better hurry. The animals are saving a special seat just for me!"

Ji-Stu arrived at the council grounds just as the others gathered around the fire. All the animals had combed and groomed their coats. Even Yona the bear was excited and smiling as he welcomed them to the contest.

"And here is our guest of honor," he announced. "Everyone find your places while Otter sits here at the center of the council."

Ji-Stu stood as tall and proud as he could. Beneath Otter's coat, he felt like a winner indeed. He walked slowly over to the seat Yona showed him, turning back and forth in the firelight as the coat glistened, so that all the animals could get a good look at him.

The animals took turns dancing around the fire and showing off their various pelts and coats. But none compared to the one worn by Ji-Stu. When his turn came, everyone cheered, and he knew that he had won.

Yona the Bear watched all the animals closely as they moved around the fire. He had to agree that Otter's coat was clearly the best of all. But there was something wrong about Otter. Why did he seem so proud and arrogant? And why did he keep holding his paw over his face?

Ji-Stu saw Yona walking toward him and thought, "This is it! Yona is coming to tell me that I am the winner. Mine is the most beautiful coat in all the forest!"

The great Bear came closer. He sniffed at the air. Yona's nose was never wrong, and a familiar sense came over him at once. It was that trickster Rabbit!

"Ji-Stu!" Yona roared and slapped Ji-Stu's paw away, revealing his face and tiny split nose. "What have you done with Otter?"

In an instant, Ji-Stu leaped as high as he could, leaving Otter's coat in a heap on the ground. But Yona was too fast for him. His long claws slashed out and grabbed Ji-Stu's tail in mid-air. Ji-Stu struggled and pulled. He wanted nothing to do with the angry Yona. And suddenly, he was free!

Ji-Stu went sailing through the crowd and into the forest before Yona could say another word. Yona began dancing around the fire as the animals gathered around him. In his clenched claws he held Ji-Stu's beloved tail.

"Look at my beautiful tail!" Yona laughed, waving the tail in the air. "Look at my beautiful tail!"

The council decided that Otter's coat was the finest one of all. Yona traveled up the river to return the coat. Thanks to Ji-Stu, Otter learned to love swimming, and he has lived in the river ever since. Yona attached Ji-Stu's tail to his rattle and took it with him to all the dances. Ji-Stu found that he could leap and run through the woods much faster without that troublesome tail. And even now, no one can catch him!